This book
BELONGS TO:

....

The GHOST in Annie's Room

The GHOST in Annie's Room

Philippa Pearce

With illustrations by Cate James

Barrington Stoke

Published in 2017 in Great Britain by
Barrington Stoke Ltd
18 Walker Street, Edinburgh, EH3 7LP

www.barringtonstoke.co.uk

A CIP catalogue record for this book is available
from the British Library upon request

ISBN: 978-1-78112-685-1

Printed in China by Leo

This book is in a super readable format for young readers
beginning their independent reading journey.

Contents

CHAPTER 1

Haunted

At first Emma Brown liked the look of the little attic bedroom.

"I thought you might like to sleep here, dear," Great Aunt Win said.

"Oh, yes!" Emma said at once.
"Thank you!"

Emma and her brother, Joe, and their parents had come to stay for three nights with Great Aunt Win in her little cottage by the sea. There was not much room for visitors.

Joe was going to sleep downstairs on a camp-bed. Mum and Dad would sleep in the spare room upstairs. And then there was the attic bedroom at the very top of the house ...

"I'm so glad you like this bedroom, dear," Great Aunt Win said to Emma. "It's a little girl's room – my little girl's room." Great Aunt Win sighed. "Oh, I still miss Annie so!"

"Who's Annie?" Emma asked.

Mum was standing beside her at the top of the attic stairs. She frowned.

"Really, Emma!" she said. "You ought to know about your cousin Annie. She was your aunty Win's little girl, long ago."

"Oh," said Emma.

Later, downstairs, when the two
children were alone, Joe said to Emma,
"You're going to sleep in the haunted
bedroom."

"Don't be stupid," said Emma.

"I'm not being stupid," Joe said. "Dad and Mum were talking, and they didn't know I could hear. They said the attic bedroom was haunted, but the ghost wouldn't do you any harm, anyway, probably."

"I don't believe you," said Emma. "How could you overhear all that?"

"I just could."

"It's all rubbish," said Emma. "I'm going to ask Mum and Dad."

"Oh, yes, you do that!" Joe jeered. "Of course they'll say there isn't a ghost, just to comfort you."

So, after that, Emma didn't ask about any ghosts in the attic bedroom. Besides, as she told herself, Joe liked to tease her. Sometimes his teases were really bad, and she hated them. Like now.

But the main thing for Emma to remember was – there was no ghost.

CHAPTER 2

The Wind

That night Emma was the first to go to bed. Great Aunt Win took her up to her bedroom.

There was a door on the landing, by the other two bedrooms. Then a steep, narrow staircase led up into the attic. It was a little room right under the roof.

At the far end was a window. A tree grew just outside. Its leaves darkened the window and filled the room with shadows. There was a bed and a dressing-table with a long mirror.

Great Aunt Win pointed out a shelf full of little china ornaments.

"Annie's china cats and kittens," she said. "She collected them when she was your age. She doted on animals. Doted." Great Aunt Win sighed.

Emma wished Great Aunt Win wouldn't sigh every time she said Cousin Annie's name.

"Here's the light switch," Great Aunt Win said more briskly. "It's rather difficult to find in the dark, so notice it now. But you won't want to put it on, once you're in bed. You'll be so cosy up here. Annie always was. She loved it."

Great Aunt Win sighed again.

Mum came to tuck Emma up for the night. "Remember, Em, if you want us, you only have to come down the stairs," she said. "When I go down, I'll leave that stair door ajar. It will stay open all night."

"But I'll be all right up here, won't I?" Emma asked.

"Of course you will," said Mum. She kissed Emma goodnight, and left her.

Emma listened to the gentle rustling of leaves just outside the attic window. After a while, she fell asleep.

She woke with a start. It seemed to be hours later. She was sure that someone had been trying to wake her by tapping at the window. Someone WAS tapping at the window.

The tapping sometimes stopped, then started again. It always started again.

And Emma was sure that there were eyes looking at her.

But through her fear she noticed another sound. A wind had risen and was blowing quite hard round the little house. It would be tossing the branches of the tree just outside her attic window. An idea came to her. Emma sat up in bed and looked towards her window.

Yes, she was right. The wind was rattling leaves and twigs against the glass. That was what had sounded like fingers tapping.

She lay back in bed. She forgot about eyes that had looked at her. She fell asleep.

By morning the wind had blown itself out.

But at breakfast Joe said, "I bet the wind was howling round your bedroom last night, Em."

"Really?" Emma said, as she munched her toast. "I slept. It's such a cosy room. I'm sorry about your camp-bed downstairs."

CHAPTER 3

In the Shadows

The blustery night was followed by a day of perfect sunshine. The Brown family spent all of it by the sea.

Emma was tired when she went to bed.

"Sleep well," Mum said, as she tucked her up.

But Emma lay awake. Suddenly she thought of the door at the bottom of the attic stairs. Had Mum remembered to leave it open? Of course, that didn't really matter, now that there wasn't a ghost.

All the same ...

Moonlight shone outside the window, but there were shadows in certain corners of the room. Emma remembered last night's feeling of being watched, and wished she hadn't remembered it. She made up her mind to get out of bed. She meant to put on the light and have a proper look round the attic, but she couldn't find the light switch.

She decided to go down the attic stairs and check that the door was still open. She felt her way down and – sure enough – it had been left open. The gap even let her hear the TV from downstairs.

So that was all right.

She climbed the stairs again to go back to bed. As she began to cross the attic floor, she was looking towards the window.

A dim figure in white was coming towards her.

It looked like a little girl. It paused, just as Emma halted.

Emma tried to open her mouth to scream, but could not. It was like a nightmare. She could make no sound. But she raised her arm to protect herself. And, from under her arm, she saw that the figure in white also raised its arm, just as she was doing. Exactly like her.

Then Emma realised what she was looking at – her own reflection in the mirror of the dressing-table!

She watched herself watching herself in the mirror. Then she went back to bed. Oddly, the feeling of watching eyes did not leave her – but she slept.

Next morning, Emma did not tell anyone of her midnight mistake. But she said to Joe, "No ghost again last night!"

He replied grumpily. "Oh, I just knew you'd believe anything!"

CHAPTER 4

Thunder and Lightning

The Browns' second day by the sea was almost as good as the first. But towards the end of it, dark clouds built up on the horizon and thunder rumbled in the distance.

Great Aunt Win worried for Emma
sleeping at the top of the house.

"I hope you're not afraid of thunder
and lightning, dear?" she asked.

"Oh, Emma's all right, aren't you,
Em?" Mum said. "It's Joe who doesn't like
it much."

Joe looked furious. Emma looked smug.

That night Emma heard the thunder coming closer in her dreams, and she woke to a flash of lightning.

She gave a little shriek, for someone really was standing in the middle of the floor.

It was Mum. "I've only come up to shut the window against the rain."

So that was all right.

Emma listened to Mum's footsteps going down the attic stairs. Now Mum would be going to check on Joe downstairs, to make sure that he was all right. He really hated thunder and lightning.

Thunder and lightning would not keep Emma awake. She settled herself to sleep again.

But she could not sleep.

Her feeling from the night before and from the night before that returned … Someone was in the room, watching her. This time she was certain of it.

"But there's no one," she said to herself.

Yet there must be.

Emma waited for the next flash of lightning. No one was there.

Yet she was sure that eyes watched her.

She forced herself to sit up in bed. There was a lull in the storm, no thunder, no lightning. She peered into the attic's shadowy corners.

Then she saw the watcher – two yellow eyes were staring at her almost from floor level.

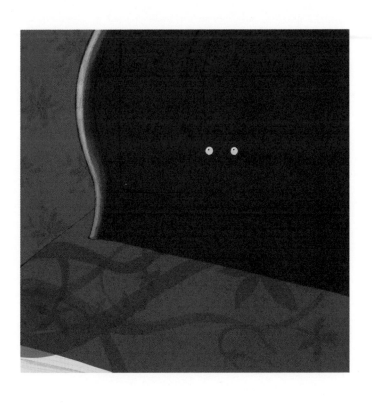

"Oh! It's a cat!" Emma called to it softly. "Puss, puss, puss!"

But the little cat – very dark, with a white front – would not come to her. It slid away among the shadows, hardly more than a shadow itself.

"Don't be afraid of the thunder and lightning," Emma whispered. "I'll look after you."

The little cat's eyes stared at her, but it would not come.

At last Emma gave up coaxing it. She lay down again to go to sleep. She wondered how the little cat had got up into the attic, but then she remembered the door left ajar. That was it.

She was dozing off again, when she heard purring from the foot of the bed. The little cat had come to her after all. It had jumped on to her duvet ...

Emma would have liked to press her feet against the cat for company, but she didn't want to scare it away. It was such a timid little thing.

"Goodnight, puss," Emma whispered. She slept.

CHAPTER 5

Little Black Cat

When Emma woke in the morning, the cat had gone.

At breakfast, Great Aunt Win asked if Emma had slept well.

"Very well, thank you, Aunty Win. I like Cousin Annie's room. Is she dead?"

"Emma!" Mum cried, shocked. "Cousin Annie is married with five children, and she lives in New Zealand."

Great Aunt Win sighed. "I miss Annie so."

Emma made a face at Joe, but he pretended not to notice.

Later, in the car, going home, Emma said, "I wanted to say goodbye to the cat."

"What cat?" Joe said. "Aunty Win hasn't got a cat."

"The little black one with a white front. It slept all night on my bed."

"She hasn't got a cat," repeated Joe.

"She has."

"She hasn't."

"Stop that," said Dad.

Mum hadn't been listening properly to the argument. Now she said, "You're both right, in a way. Aunty hasn't got a cat. But long ago, when Cousin Annie was a little girl, she had a little black cat with a white front. Aunty Win showed me a photo of them together. And ... she said the cat always slept at the bottom of Annie's bed. Just as you said, Emma."